Mowa Popins and the Golden Necklace

And Other Short Stories

Enaya Agrawal

ukiyoto®

Ukiyoto Publishing

All global publishing rights are held by

Ukiyoto Publishing

Published in 2020

Content Copyright © **Enaya Agrawal**

ISBN 9789367957677

All rights reserved.

No part of this publication may be reproduced, transmitted, or stored in a retrieval system, in any form by any means, electronic, mechanical, photocopying, recording or otherwise, without the prior permission of the publisher.

The moral right of the author has been asserted.

This book is sold subject to the condition that it shall not by way of trade or otherwise, be lent, resold, hired out or otherwise circulated, without the publisher's prior consent, in any form of binding or cover other than that in which it is published. Any person who does any unauthorised act in relation to this publication may be liable to criminal prosecution and civil claims for damages.

To Mumma, Papa and Didi without whom I would have never been able to come this far.

CONTENTS

Mowa Popins and the Golden Necklace	*1*
The Jaws of Doom	*25*
The Crooked Castle and I	*27*
Sita's Birthday	*30*
The Hero	*33*
Fairy Folk	*35*
All Because of Albania	*39*
About the Author	***42***

Mowa Popins and the Golden Necklace

Once upon a time, in a land far far away, the monsters and dragons lived happily ever after. Or so I thought. It all began 200 years ago. Everyone was happy and cheerful till the day the golden necklace, which was supposed to be responsible for choosing the next ruler of the country, was stolen. Both parties blamed the other for the disappearance and thus, there was a crack in their friendship. The dragons went away and settled on one end of the world. Ever since, the monsters and dragons don't meet eye to eye. Legend says, no king can die without the permission of the necklace, and thus, since that day, the same king, the one with the deep gray and almost comical body of a donkey and a long, giraffe head that is rumored to reach the clouds at its full length, has been ruling over the country. The king is old, and his tall head is always bent with the weight of his burden. Many people have tried to kill him but failed because of the power of the golden necklace.

I am Mowa Poppins, a monster with a cat's head and the body of a panda, and I live in this post-dragonala era (a world where monsters and dragons are not friends). My friends call me Blue, because my eyes and fur are ocean colored. The word 'Monster' was extracted from the verb which means 'to warn'. Its noun form, 'monstrum' means 'evil omen' but that doesn't mean that we are grimmy. Humans probably think that we are dangerous and boorish but as per my knowledge, we are friendly creatures who have no intentions of harming humans. In fact, all other monsters except me are scared of humans. How funny is it that, humans and monsters are scared of each other? In our world, we don't talk of the golden necklace or the dragons. And frankly, I couldn't be less bothered! I go to my school POP the Great that admits monsters from all around the country. It is the most prestigious institution of its kind with classes on our history, ways to discover our superpowers and ways to enhance our animal bodies. I don't like my school much, but my hardworking parents who have government jobs have worked hard to afford this school for me, and I don't want to let them down. My cupboard is full of second-hand things starting from my school uniform to my socks. I love the flavor of the off white colored screaming cheese berries when I am happy and laughing meatballs when I am sad. They are my all-time favorites. I don't like eating screaming cheese berries because of their high pitch noise. Just when I am about to put them in my mouth, they make those adorable watery eyes, and if I still decide to eat them, I am startled by their wailing in the middle of my meal. However, laughing meatballs always cheer me up with their enthusiastic laughs whenever I am sad. It is filled with cheese inside which I find tempting to eat. I like gardening and painting in my free time. We have a garden full of Montrees (talking monster trees) which need a regular supply of lava to grow healthily, and my parents put me in charge of it. I often need to go out to the shop to buy lava for the magnificent Montrees. They are huge and bear fruits throughout the year. Montrees don't bear leaves like the other trees. There are ten hours a day here, which means that we eat only two meals a day. I need to lava Montrees three times daily to maintain the garden. Accompanying our garden is my creepy old house which is also government property. I don't like my house either because I never know where the rooms will be, since they're always changing positions. Once I needed to go to the washroom urgently, but the weird house changed its position and made me run around the whole house to find it!

Oh, did I mention my special powers are night vision and transforming my teacher into a snail whenever I want to? Yes, you read it right. I get to do that at monster school! How amazing is that? Oh also don't tell anybody about the snail thing they don't know yet and my parents would kill me if they knew I have been doing that to teachers all along.

There have been rumors about war with the dragons lately. I have never seen the city go so wild. Montrees in the garden keep whispering, the adults keep having their "secret" meetings where I can hear them eat screaming cheese berries. I barely even get to see my parents anymore! Someone at school told me the dragons will invade soon. Something about this fight has kept me up nights. My creepy old house is more noisy than usual. Whispers keep reaching from the walls but I can never make out what they are really saying.

One morning, I woke to the sound of my alarm clock only to realize that summer vacation had started! I could at last sleep in. I felt relieved and laid back on my cozy bed which was currently playing terrifying stories. The blue colored bed on which I sleep was gifted to me by my uncle. It is oval-shaped and very comfortable. At night, it automatically starts narrating a story about monsters when I lay down on it. Have you ever experienced sleeping after listening to a long fable about monsters? If not, then please try it this night itself and let the ghosts and monsters haunt you in your bedroom.

I slept uninterrupted for a whole another hour, till I heard my mother loudly praying and singing. All the noise woke me up completely, so I got up and off I went to the bathroom. My morning routine included brushing my teeth with the brown Nasty Breath toothpaste and then munching on some soft and plump Monsterberry cereal. It had all my favorite things; poisonous strawberry with gooseberry punch, mango with shiny pearls, and tiny little marshmallows. It consisted of millions of flavors and said the flavor's name when the delicious cereals started melting in my mouth.

This is when I heard mom crying downstairs. I listened through the walls into their bedroom as I couldn't bear mom crying and the alligators in her tears polluting our room. You see, I also have really good ears. They help when I want to eavesdrop. Mom was talking about leaving town. Dad was furious. They were both very frustrated since they had been working non-stop. I myself had not seen them for more than a few minutes all week! I resolved to take matters into my own hands.

I started thinking about the war as I returned to my food. Why wasn't the government doing something about it? What if the dragons attack us? Did the golden necklace still exist? I obviously didn't want a war. Our side should do something right?!

I decided to wait. Surely the government had something planned. I waited and waited, watching the news on the windowpane but days started to pass by and I could see progress. My parents started staying away for longer, and in the evenings, more and more alligators started reaching my room. I completely lost faith in the government and decided to try to find some clues myself.

I munched on the brown Know-more breads which usually made my mind run fast but they seemed to do nothing at the moment. Eventually, I made up my mind to go out and find a clue about the fabled necklace instead of sitting and eating at home to help end the war, and also because it sounded really cool! Finding a clue about the golden necklace would obviously not be a simple task. Years had gone and professionals had failed in the quest. I wouldn't just find it lying on the road. I thought of wandering the bloody skeleton filled street, but searching near my house was futile. Oh, you must be wondering about the streets. You see, the streets in the monster world have some or the other decorations done all the time according to the street name.

The street in which I live is called Deadly Shimmer so all the decorations are deadly there like skeletons and bloody baron. For the necklace, I searched near the king's house. It was a tough job because the house continuously kept calling out in its hoarse voice that a thief was spying on him, and worse, not even letting me touch it. Well, you guessed it right, all the houses here can speak, laugh, play and sing but they are useless if somebody wants to gather information about someone or something. They all vary in color and have two windows on either side as their eyes, and a door at the bottom through which they speak. As they grow older, they become feeble, irritable, moody and that is why monsters are forced to change their houses. I don't know why they are said to be one of the wisest creatures in the monster world. My house has never said a word that even makes sense. It is always just grunting and speaking jargon.

When I returned home all exhausted and puzzled that night, I saw some of our stuff already out to get packed. Fear set in. I didn't want to leave town! What about having fun at school (no matter how much I disliked studying it was a great place), and Timmy, my best friend in the world, and all the teachers I hadn't turned into snails yet! Going through the picture albums put out by mom, I saw an image of my grandfather remembering something strange about him all of a sudden. My grandfather was said to die in an accident, but the circumstances surrounding his death had always been very mysterious.

I was reminded of the gift he had given me when I was four years old. He had told me to open it when I needed it the most. I hadn't understood his cryptic language then, but I had always saved it for a really important occasion. Today, I thought it was the right time to open it since I really didn't want to move away from town and I needed something to solve the mystery about the golden necklace. I remembered the box very well. It was a small wooden cuboid with rough edges made up of steel. It had no decoration except a big gemstone placed on its top. I remember carefully putting the box in my locker years ago. I hastily rushed towards my room for the locker now.

It took four tries but I finally found my room. As soon as I opened the locker, it asked me for a three-line code in cat language. The only language I knew by birth was cat language. I whispered the password and it swung open. I could see the small leather box inside it, but when I took it out and tried to open the lock it started to cry out loudly like a little baby. In not more than a second its behavior changed. now it had transformed from the cranky little baby to a furious man sucking and biting my finger. I almost felt my finger burning into ash from the hot flames it started giving out. When it finally let go of my finger, I let out a high pitched wail. I had never seen such a strange monster in my life, not even my friend Timmy had the talent to do this. Now all I needed was a key to open the box and find out what was inside it. I could not remember my grandpa giving me a key but I figured it must be lying somewhere in the house. Grandpa tended to forget things very quickly and I simply guessed he had forgotten to give me the key. Now the task at hand seemed brutal. Looking for a key in this enormous door changing house would be like looking for a needle in a haystack. Tired and spent out of my wits, I decided to call it a day and resume my search the next morning. I barely slept that night as well, constantly getting woken by the loud whispers and nightmares about moving away.

I woke up the next morning and immediately started hunting for the key in my room. The key could be lying anywhere, grandpa was not good at keeping things in the right place either. I rolled over the colorful slimy carpet so that my leg could not stick on it. This was another gift from my uncle. I usually tried not to step on the carpet as anything could easily stick to it. I had loved to prank and play with it as a child. I reminiscenced my days as a kid as I searched the bedside, dusty shelves, yelling cushions, inside the water tank and every place I could think of, but to my great disappointment, I was unable to find any sort of key. It was almost evening and my room looked like a total disaster. All my things were either yelling or screaming at me for troubling them or lying on the ground. Sometimes living in a monster world can be annoying because most of the things have a voice- kinda puts a bummer on the whole activism thing but believe me objects speaking is irritating and annoying.

I looked over my shoulder at the leather box which was kept on the shelf. I was really eager to know what hid inside it. I spent the other half of the day searching other places in the house that I knew of, like my parent's bedroom, the living room and the bathroom. You'll be surprised to know that I have lived in this house for as long as I can remember, but never have I managed to memorize all the rooms and chambers since they keep switching. I tried my best to look for the key.

At long last, I gave up on the search for the key and started thinking of other ways to find a lead that would help me find the golden necklace. Absently, I went out in the garden and brought one of my favorite vegetables, which was none other than Smelly graved potatoes, into the house. My mother had assigned me this task so that she could bake them for dinner. These potatoes had the ability to act like the person who had grown them. My yard's potatoes kept on giggling and sometimes singing like my mother since she had grown them. When I was done collecting the potatoes and was heading back to my house, something unexpected happened. My house greeted me! Now you might think it is normal for monster houses to greet their residents, and normally it would be. But you see, my house had never done this before in all the years I had lived here. Whenever I passed by it, it seemed to be sleeping.

Hesitantly, I wished it back and now it broke off into a whole poem. Its grim voice sounded like it was shaking off cobwebs and hadn't been used in a while. Subconsciously, it seemed to resemble grandpa's voice

It said,

"All embed owe yore

Ee more ta yore cont pont ya

Aal diow royano yore cornt oolah ustanta oolohh"

It was speaking in the monster language and nothing was going inside my head, so I gave it a confused look.

It huffed, blowing dust all over my body, and then translated,

"What you have been looking for is with you.

It's just that you can't see it.

At dusk, 013 you will feel the ray of sunshine in your shine."

I stood there shocked. No one else had been witness to the sound since my parents as usual had gone off to work and I was home alone.

Slowly, it opened the door and let me in the house. I put the potatoes in the kitchen for dinner and went inside my room, bewildered.

I thought for what seemed like hours. What did the house mean? Is it a clue for me to find the key? What did it mean by dusk 013? Is it a room in this house that it is talking about? I was as confused as a newly born Rhinobird (Rhinobirds are multicolored and always confusing in nature) and slept all exhausted without having dinner.

I woke up to the startling sound of television and found that it was almost dusk and I had been sleeping for nearly a day. Mother had forgotten to wake me up. I felt weak and tired as I had not eaten anything since breakfast, the previous day. I dashed to the dining table where my mother had kept my breakfast. She also asked me to take a bath since I had not taken one for 25 days. But today was no day for baths. The war threats had increased and I wanted to do something at the earliest.

I had to find room 013 and reach there before dusk. I wanted to try what the house had suggested as soon as possible. I gobbled up my breakfast and then went to look for the key which I guessed was in a room called 013. I didn't even know if it even existed.

I looked through my half-packed stuff mom had insisted I put together for the I-know-the-way slippers. They really did seem to know the way and took me to the topmost floor and through a small door. God, I love these slippers! Mom and Dad had given the pair to me on my birthday last year. It was a family heirloom that grandpa had bought from somewhere years back and had performed a magical spell that made them memorize every route of this confusing house. I was surprised to see the dirty wide glass windows which stood just like a wall around the room. It was dark in there, the only source of light was the setting sun. It looked as if the room had not been cleaned for a 100 years. Midora's spooky webs (our friendly neighborhood spider) were all around the corners. I accidentally tripped over one and spotted what I had been looking for since many hours. The key! It was stuck on the web. I managed to take it out. It did not wail or cry, it was just like an ordinary key dipped in mouth warming monster flavored cheese Monchhes. It was made up of gold and had a big diamond stud fitted on top.

Turning the key in the box's lock, a transparent mudpap (monster paper) floated in midair with the light of the setting sun. I went near the mudpap to take a closer look and was astonished to see that it was a letter from my grandfather. The handwriting was not that clear but somehow I managed to read it.

Dear grandson,

I hope that your cat eyes are not causing you any trouble reading this. I am glad that the old house let you know the clue. However, I want you to know something eminently important. When I was giving you the box I was just going to put in some of our family's heirlooms, but then I found out something tragic and changed my mind.

With a heavy heart, I have to inform you that the Great King under whom we have worked all these years and who has provided us with this house of his to live in has poisoned me. The king whom we all worshipped has betrayed me and I want you to avenge me. This house once belonged to the king. He assured the people that the dragons stole the necklace and rented me this house in which he hid the necklace. When I found out his secret and the place where the necklace hid, he tried to poison me. I am using my last breaths to write this letter to you.

I want you to return the necklace to the dragon king. To get the necklace all you need to do is go to the painting of the king on the wall and say 'Pinocullous' and take out the necklace. Don't tell anybody about this. Remember, this letter is written in heirograph, so it will disappear once the sun sets on the day you touch it.

All the best son! May you always stink!

Love

Michael Popins (grandpa)

After reading the letter, at first, I was in shock! Our king killed our granddad? I always thought they were the best of friends. No wonder he overworks my parents and they are scared for their life and want to move out! Now things started to get clearer in my mind. I understood how badly the King wanted to live longer and how he poisoned my grandfather by telling us that he got a stroke while working. The king hid the necklace in his house so that it would be difficult for anybody to find it (the changing doors really suck). This also explains why the house seemed to be upset all the time. What I had been searching for all this while had been here all along.

Everything in the letter made sense to me, except there was one problem. The painting was missing! The king must have taken the painting with him after he poisoned my grandpa. This case was getting critical and if I needed to unearth the mystery, I needed to get help. So I asked my best friend and classmate- Timmy, the person I trust the most in the whole world, to help me. I told him everything I knew so far and he immediately agreed, but on one condition- I laughed at his every joke for a month! You see, he wants to be a comedian when he grows up. I obliged.

After our discussion, we focused on finding the painting, which we assumed would still be inside the monster house, the king's residence. With the horrible experiences I had had visiting that house, I really did not want to visit it. But this time, we went with a contingency plan. We managed to disguise ourselves in crimson clothes as two of the staff members in the monster palace. (Timmy's idea). Even the house had no excuse to stop us from going inside. We planned to go inside and work as a normal monster staff while trying to find the painting. I was sure nobody would be able to recognize us since we were all covered in staff robes.

And so we went in. The monster house was magnificent. All around us we saw millions of monster staff busy working, probably because it was the cleaning hours of the castle since the king was out. I watched in awe and fascination as some monsters cleaned the freaky bedroom which had a huge ceiling so that the king could stand tall without bumping his head. No-one seemed to be bothered with anyone around them. They all minded their own business as all types of monsters around the house worked in different chambers.

I saw a room filled with millions of paintings at a corner, and my heart literally skipped a beat. Timmy was just going to start his investigation when we heard a loud Ting-Tong. It was a sign the staff had to leave. The working hour was up, and the king was going to arrive soon. All the staff there were trained to clean the house before the king arrived and thus, they started filing as we turned to leave.

Timmy complained, "Blue, now what? We didn't even get the time to look for the painting. We hardly spent fifteen minutes in the house."

"Don't worry we can come back tomorrow on time. For now, let's go to your house and get some breakfast. All this spying has made me famished.", I suggested.

We decided to take a Hornride to Timmy's house since it was miles away as neither of us had the stamina to walk. They were the cheapest vehicles on the road but we still couldn't afford them. But the thought of walking all the way home was unbearable. We stopped one of the colorful vehicles (Hornrides are the only vehicles in all types of colors) as we dreamt of hearing music on their radio all the way home. The cart was pulled over and the Hornist- a four-legged creature- popped his head out. The Hornride drivers usually accept Montlacs, the general currency of our country.

"Please take us to Deadly Shimmer, street number 4", I practically begged.

The driver sighed, probably tired of hearing this. He nodded, and then said, "Do you have Montlacs, kids?" Oh crap! Montlacs, our general currency. Timmy and I had already spent the last of our monthly allowance on Monsterberry last week!

We exchanged looks with each other. Timmy assured the driver that we would surely pay him once we reached Timmy's house. Oof! that would be a difficult task. The driver obliged, and we hurriedly jumped in, almost seeming to forget everything about the necklace after hearing the melody playing on the ride.

After fifteen bouncy minutes, we reached Timmy's house. Timmy's mother seemed to be in a good mood, so it did not take very long convincing her to cover for us.

"We will repay you tomorrow but for now please give us 3 montlacs", we both said in unison.

"Hold your horses boys. One at a time. You need not repay me, I am just messing around with you." said Timmy's mother in amusement.

As soon as the Hornride left, we dashed into Timmy's dining room while greeting his father. His mother, who was a good chef, had prepared Bloody Baron soup for lunch which was utterly delicious. After the meal, we were on our way to Timmy's room to discuss the next day's plans, when the bell rang and a strange person in sharp horns and a coat entered the house. He had a peculiar behavior about him. But we were in a hurry, so we didn't pay any attention, eagerly making our way to the room to discuss tomorrow's plans. Once inside, we came up with all kinds of ideas and situations.

It was almost midnight by the time we were done and so I chose to hurry home to avoid my mother's fury.

Timmy dropped me home since it was right beside Deadly Shimmer street number 3. We vowed to meet again in the morning outside the monster house.

The next morning we had flying Tropas together for breakfast at my house. We faced a little trouble with them since they continued to fly away in the shape of a paper plane making a "Weeee' sound, but we managed. Timmy reasoned that facing the trouble was worth it because they were extremely delicious-and food fights were fun. After breakfast, we got dressed as workers for our visit to the monster house again. As we sneaked out, my parents saw us, but to our surprise, they agreed to let us go out. I assumed they had a lot on their minds, making my grit to fix this issue stronger. This time, we walked to the house and didn't bother wasting our precious time exploring. We headed straight to the painting room which was massive with paintings lying all over the floor, ceiling, and walls. There were all types and sizes of paintings hung across the walls depicting phenomena, pop culture and what they call "abstract" art. I could clearly see how passionate the royal family was about artists.

Timmy kept saying, "I found it" whenever he saw a painting of a king. There were about a million paintings there, especially of Kings but we had to find the one with the body of a donkey and the head of a giraffe. It wasn't as easy as I had thought. Time flew by and we were soon very exhausted. Seeing our condition, it almost looked like we had been working with the other monster staff all this time. Timmy still didn't give up, determined to find the painting while I sulked in a corner. "Come on, we don't have enough time. The bell will ring exactly 12 minutes from now," he said in an exaggerated voice.

I was exhausted and decided I would lie down and close my eyes for a few minutes. Just as I was about to doze off, Timmy started shaking me, trying to give me the good news. My heart skipped a beat: right in front of me stood a rectangular painting of a monster who had the body of a donkey and the head of a giraffe, the painting of the king! It was on top of a pile of paintings and looked too old to even exist. I admired the royalty. The Great King of Monster stood there with a chest swollen with pride. He was wearing a red coat while his hands and neck were full of expensive jewelleries. The crown that he wore had a big diamond in the center. Without even thinking for a minute my mouth spat 'Pinoculous' and suddenly a square shape cut right through the painting's head. Timmy turned towards me and saw me putting my hand inside the square hole. He jumped out of his pants when I pulled out THE GOLDEN NECKLACE. It was long and had the charm of the monster parliament hanging from it. The symbol of the monster parliament consisted of a monster standing under the shade of a dragon's great wings. This is used to represent the dragons' and monsters' friendship. I squealed with joy. That was proof we had actually FOUND IT! I won't have to move. I can save us all. My parents won't be overworked. I was elated. I quickly stuffed the necklace in my pocket, careful so no-one would notice. I made sure that it was properly secured. I couldn't believe that we had ultimately managed to find the necklace after so many days of hard work. All thanks to my grandpa, I would have never come this far otherwise. Almost on cue, the bell rang and we rushed out, treating ourselves to a Hornride again. My heart was racing as I put the necklace safely in the locker with grandpa's letter but neither of them could stop Timmy from cracking his joke, "Knock, knock. Who's there? Cargo. Cargo who? Car go, "Toot toot, vroom, vroom. I had to stop myself from facepalming as I remembered my promise. He really had been a huge help. God knows what I'd do without him.

It was a usual Sunday afternoon. Rhinobirds were chirping, the sun was up and everything seemed normal until my father turned on the national news channel. A half-faced ashen eyed monster was reporting the news, it said, "THE WAR IS BACK BETWEEN THE MONSTERS AND THE DRAGONS". The Dragons have almost crossed the Great Wall of Maniacs. Our fellow Moniers (monster soldiers) are at the border struggling to keep them out. Keep your doors locked and 'Piranha Launchers'- works just like I sound- ready for firing." I hated Pirana Launchers and had only ever seen them twice before since they were only brought out during Emergencies. But I had to agree they were exceedingly powerful and the only weakness of the dragons. Sometimes we had troubles with Piranhas coming out of their launchers but it was okay as long as they didn't bite us.

Several questions took the empty space in my mind, What was the Great King Of Monsters doing? How long will the Moniers be able to keep out the dragons? What will happen if they take over our city? My thoughts were interrupted with a frightening scream which seemed to be coming from outside, but we could not see anything happening outside since all the doors as well as curtains, and windows had been closed by my parent's instructions. All sorts of creepy noises I had never heard before came to life. My mother tried to stop me but I just could not bear it anymore. I pulled the door open, just to see our neighborhood getting killed. Tears stung my eyes to see monsters suffering and screaming. Dragons were throwing fireballs at them and even the Piranha Launchers weren't working. The Dragons had returned and this time they seemed stronger than monsters. My heart sank seeing the city ruined, smoke blowing over the hills and houses as everything was set on fire. Nothing was visible at the other end of the city except dragons flying in the sky and smoke coming out of the torched houses. At dawn, it was clear that the city was no longer safe for us to live in. I resolved I had to return the necklace to the dragon king immediately.

But how? If I went searching for him in the city it would be too late and no one would survive. Nothing seemed to come to mind. I stood with the necklace in a complete panic, placing it near my heart as a protective measure. I wished for the dragon king to take back the necklace and stop the war. I wished, "OH dragon king, wherever you are please receive this present from me and stop the war." trying to manifest for the universe to give me a direction for help. In the blink of an eye, the necklace disappeared in a golden mist and everything seemed peaceful. The dragons halted where they were and the monsters stopped crying. The Dragon King was suddenly standing in front of me wearing the golden necklace. He was a huge red colored dragon with enormous wings. His nose breathed fire, his teeth were keen and broad. Staring at the enormous Dragon King, I thought I was dreaming. Timmy came running from his house and pinched me to confirm this was real.

"Thank you for returning back the necklace. Before I take any further decisions, I need to know all about your journey in finding this necklace," he said in his booming but kind voice. He seemed astonished it was school kids who had ended the war.

Timmy and I explained all about the letter and the painting to my parents, Timmy's parents, and the Dragon King. When we had finished, he said, "I appreciate your courage, and you will surely be rewarded. Now please excuse me. I am running short of time and need to put that traitor in the Haunted house." He opened his wide wings and flew back in the air as we stood and watched in awe. The Haunted House was considered to be the scariest thing in the monster world- a type of a prison here. Demented monsters were found there. It was said flying ghosts and trolls haunted every prisoner's dream there. Surviving there was the toughest punishment any monster could ever get. No one ever came out the same-if at all- from there. I shuddered at the thought.

The next day, the king of dragons invited us to the monster house where he told us that The Great King of Monsters had been sent to the haunted house. The golden necklace had now announced the new king of the monsters- WHO ARE ME AND TIMMY! The necklace decided to change history by announcing two of the youngest kings ever. We now have the power of the golden necklace upon ourselves. Timmy couldn't believe his ears when the Dragon King told him this himself. Me? I hurt myself pinching.

He said, "Come on King don't play jokes on me. I am honestly good at cracking jokes and I don't expect you to do this."

"Don't be on your high horse Timmy", I whispered from the corner of my mouth. I was sure that we were going to get into some sort of trouble because of Timmy's behavior but contrary to what I had thought, the King was so pleased with us that he was not cross with Timmy. in fact, he invited us to his country to spend the summer.

Timmy and I now have millions of Moniers and staff working under us who do exactly what we instruct them. We can eat whatever and whenever we want to. No one can stop us except, of course, our family.

The council understood our need to live with our parents and go to school as we were still kids. I am proud to state that I made my first ever decision as a king to stay at home with my family instead of the monster house (we do visit it often but mostly stay at home). I thanked the old house for being kind to me and telling me the clue. Can you believe this? I changed history, the dragons and monsters are friends once again! The dragon king agreed to live like we used to 200 years ago on the condition that as they have worked hard to build a whole new city at the other end of the world, they will stay there and manage everything on Motobyles (telephone).

This time, I am sure that the monsters and dragons will live happily ever after.

The Jaws of Doom

Mickey Watson and Snowy Halls, two 13-year-olds, unknowingly walked across the Bomario Gangzon in Mexico. The night was dark, nobody except them was fond of going inside The Jaws of Doom- A cave which had a dense and broad mouth covered with buzzing bats. It had two hollow sockets for eyes occupied by shining owls. The holes for the nose breathed nothing but fire. The two friends always looked forward to finding adventures and when they had the opportunity to go inside the world's most haunted place, how could they miss it?

Mickey followed by Snowy passed the fleet of bats with great difficulty. The inside was piled up with skeleton heads and spider webs, hanging from the ceiling. A nasty smell filled the cave. It was the skulled man of Bomario Gangzon. Mickey and Snowy started shivering with fright at the sight since they had heard haunted stories about the skulled man. The skulled man was no far from a foot, he had a gross skull which was half-covered with blood and mud. He looked much thinner than they had expected. Snowy thought that the skulled man's body was detachable and he had not taken a bath in a hundred years. The skulled man walked towards them and said, "Welcome to the jaws of doom, nobody has ever managed to leave this place alive! Let's see if you can!" Before Mickey and Snowy could even move the skulled man whispered something. 'THUD' a large sound echoed suddenly and the whole cave lit up.

A thousand miles away, Tom Hood woke up, panicking and assuming that he was next.

The Crooked Castle and I

Where was I? The last thing I remember was defending my home from invaders. Now I was stiff and cold. It was hard to breathe. I pushed and shoved, there was a ripping and tearing, suddenly I was blinded by the light...

It was a wintery morning and snow was drizzling over the grounds of Harvard. I was inside our little cottage with my family. It had two rooms which were not bigger than a closet. However, everybody in the village was tensed. Our little village was in the midst of war. The Egyptians could attack us anytime now. We all were quivering with fear. Nobody could find a way to save our small village. Only a miracle could help us from the war.

Soon, our wildest dream came to life and the hideous 'Mummies' and 'Sphinx' (the Egyptian creatures) started attacking our village. There were millions of them and we were only 100. We tried our best to defeat the Mummies but the Sphinx were stubborn. Hours passed by and to my disappointment, our people started to die. I wanted to do something, but what? Where could I go for help? To my delight, I remembered the crooked castle ten miles away from where the solution of all problems laid. I had heard many stories about it but nobody seemed to know who lived there and how all the problems were solved. I thought that it would be best to go and find some help instead of doing nothing. I quickly prepared myself to leave. I ran as fast as my tired feet could carry me and stopped right in front of a huge tree.

The castle bore spine trees all around it and a huge fleet of bats constantly buzzed over it. It looked ruined and haunted. It was excruciatingly painful for me to pass the spine trees since many of the spines got inside my skin. Once I was outside the door of the castle I could feel a power dragging me to the topmost floor. In a wink of an eye, I was facing a golden-haired doll sitting beside a windowpane and wearing a dress made up of diamonds. I couldn't believe my eyes, the legend had been true, it was this doll who had the solution to all the problems. Before I could even move the doll was forcing her hand to lift and bring me a muddy glass containing pale liquid, although it seemed like she remained still. When I got the glass, I could feel her eyes urging me to drink. As soon as the first sip of that liquid went down my throat, the webbed room seemed to exchange its look with the battlefield. My body felt heavier than it used to. I felt too tired to even move. When I finally managed to glance at my hands and feet through the pain, I realized that I had turned into a troll with nasty breath and robes! I could feel my body weigh more than a hundred pounds. Without thinking I started to lift up the Sphinx and mummies and throw them on the ground. Before I realized, some Spinx had caught my leg and had started to bite me. My body could not bear any more pain and I started to drool. Suddenly darkness filled my eyes and I completely lost my senses.

Sita's Birthday

One fine morning, Sita woke up realizing that it was her birthday and she had just turned 10. Sita was a sweet little girl who was appreciated for her beauty by everyone. She lived with her Aai in a small cottage at Pritampura.

Running, she went to her three best friends Shami, Rupvati and Neelu to test them and see if they remembered her birthday. Carrying a sugar cane stick on her shoulders, she went all the way between the tall grass to greet her friends. Neelu was spotted nearby helping his father with the harvest, Shami was found helping her mother in chores and Rupvati as always was sitting under the tree reading a book. The four of them gathered under the cool shade of a mango tree.

"Guys, look I have been reading this wonderful book about climate change. It's called The Cloud Called Bhura.", began Rupvati. "I heard Bhaiya talk about this one.", added Neelu.

"Oh, I don't understand why everyone in your family loves to read books except you Neelu.", teased Shami.

"Stop it now!", roared Sita surprised to see that her friends had totally forgotten her birthday.

"By the way, what day is today?", Sita asked sarcastically.

"Tuesday?" "Thirteenth?" "November?", the three of them beamed in unison. She thought to herself that they were messing around with her and would come back later to wish her.

They played hopscotch, hide and seek, lock and key, passing the parcel and it was almost evening by the time they finished playing. All they did was play and by now Sita had lost all hopes that her friends or family would remember her birthday. Devastated, she deemed it the worst birthday ever. "This is the worst birthday ever. Nobody, not even Aai has wished me or given gifts.", she said to herself.

She was boiling with frustration and anger by the time they were playing aeroplane fly.

"Crow fly" "Monkey fly" "Neelu fly" "Rupvati's books fly" "Sparrow sit" and all their fingers went up and down accordingly. "My birthday fly", screamed Sita at the top of her voice. Everyone stopped at once and gaped at her for a few moments until she burst into tears. Her friends had actually forgotten her birthday. "No-body-cares fur-mmee-yo all-furgott my-birthday", she stammered. Shami tried to comfort her while Neelu started plucking out ripe mangoes from the tree. He said, "Sita, it is true that we almost forgot your birthday but do you remember it happened to me too? Now there is no point spoiling the rest of your birthday, let's have a mango party. What do you say Rupvati?" When they all agreed they had a blast and promised each other to never forget each other's birthday ever again. They also invited Manju Mami, Sheetal mausie and Chowkidar Bhaiya over. The seven of them cracked jokes and danced around the bonfire for several hours. It was both a sad and gleeful day for Sita but she could never forget it.

The Hero

Late that night, the hero Halsa and the villain Stevious were out on the street.

For the first time in his life, Halsa wanted to turn and run.

He pivoted a second too late, however, and Stevious caught his eye before he could duck into the nearest alleyway.

"Fancy seeing you here", Stevious grinned as he walked up behind Halsa, following him. "What are - hold on a second."

Halsa gritted his teeth. "What?"

"It's hot and humid, and yet you're trembling."

"I'm not," Halsa objected.

"I am not blind I can see you shaking. And what's that on your - Have you been drugged?"

"None of your damn business."

Stevious grimaced. "Let me help you." Then, upon seeing Halsa's stubborn glare, grimaced added, "Please"

Halsa was silent for a mere moment, then forced Stevious to lunge forwards as he crumbled unconscious into his arms.

BOOM, Halsa had been tricked. Stevious used his superpowers to make Halsa fall into a deep unconscious sleep. He successfully killed the hero who was to be awarded to defeat every villain in the town, but, unfortunately, lost against this ugly cunning villain. There seemed to be no scope of the last hero of the town to wake up and save the city. A huge crowd gathered around, after all, Halsa had been the citizen's last ray of hope. Not willing to stay there and listen to the gasps of people, Stevious ran away with Halsa in his hands. Far away, he went to an unruly forest situated near a lake and kept the great hero by his side.

"What should I do? he wondered. Take this young fellow to the minister and get paid or leave him here to rot to death?."

Stevious had been in confusion when suddenly black clouds started gathering in the sky blocking the moon. A bolt of lightning came crashing down and hit Halsa in the chest. His body started trembling from head to toe and he woke up with a sudden jerk, once again ready to fight.

He had a great time watching the look on Stevious's face to see him come alive. His superpower had failed against him.

The lightning was just like a miracle that saved Halsa and the city. Had it not taken place, the whole city would be in a great mayhem.

Fairy Folk

"It's that time of the year when fairy folk come to dance upon the earth. So everyone should light up the way for them, beneath the ancient tree. If you remain still, you might get a glimpse of them. Be careful though, if they suspect a trap they will grab you and imprison your soul into the tree for a 1000 years.", said the notice board at our school. But will my friend Grane agree to this and do as instructed?

Our school is one of the oldest in the country and believes that every year in August fairy folk come upon earth and pay a visit to two chosen people. How stupid can this be? Grane undoubtedly was eagerly willing to see the fairies. Not knowing exactly the night when the folk fairies will come, he wanted to sit under the tree all night for 30 days. Most of the children were planning to do the same thing. Most of them had lost their belief in fairies since no human had seen fairies for years and the ones who had were unwilling to disclose any secrets. Everyone just assumed they were lying.

Considering Grane's excitement, I too had prepared a night bag with a torch, some chocolates for nibbling, a sleeping bag and a knife for protection. Afterall I had to accompany Grane. Finally the sun dawned and we slipped over to the place over the hill where fairies were said to be seen. Many children were already there keeping a sharp eye at their surroundings. We gossiped for a while, till everyone got tired. We realised that it was getting late and we should get some sleep to make it in time for school the next day. I was half sleeping while Grane was patrolling around. When no sign of the fairies were seen, I started to feel stupid. Soon the sun was up and it was morning. We went back home all depressed and sad. After taking a shower, having our breakfast, going to school and coming back all tired, everyone prepared once again for another night of camping out. This routine remained the same for a couple of weeks. I always made excuses to not go but Grane somehow managed to take me. All the days we were there, no sign of the fairies could be seen.

All children except Grane had lost faith in fairies. After a few days, children started to go away and soon just me and Grane were left behind camping out every night. Grane still forced me to go to the hill but on the 30th of August something different happened. To my surprise, Grane as usual came into my house to take me but instead said, "You were right, the fairies are just a myth. We will never be able to see them. It's almost the end of August, it's no use for us to go back up there." I was astonished to hear Grane say this. This time I decided to hold on to him and asked him not to clam up. Contrary to what we did everyday, I pulled Grane to the top of the hill that night. No one was there, we sat under the tree attentive, looking for the fairies. It looked like Grane and I had exchanged places for a day, he was sleeping while I was looking for some sign of the fairies.

In the middle of the night, a startling noise woke me up "SHARRRRR". Before I could judge, what looked like shimmering fairies were coming out of a huge old tree's trunk. I hurriedly nudged Grane in excitement and he woke up with a startle. Carefully, and without making any noise we tried to hide behind a tree as we watched in immense glee. The sight of seeing fairy creatures dancing around a bonfire was incredible. Who would not like watching little small shiny creatures flying all around a forest? The fairy folk were shimmering blue in absolute darkness and peace. I turned my head around for Grane, who was watching with his mouth open wide. I was aching to go and talk to the fairies but I suddenly remembered the notice board, "If you remain still, you might get a glimpse of them. Be careful though. If they suspect a trap they will grab you and imprison your soul in the tree for 1000 years." I had been lucky enough to catch a glimpse of the fairies but going near them could be more dangerous for us than it seemed. Who knows when a beautiful fairy could transform into a hideous witch? Living in a tree for a 1000 years was definitely not a good idea. Something in the wind told me that I should not mention these fairies to any one. Grane who still watched with his mouth wide open was completely adoring the beautiful bonfire sight. I decided to tell him what I felt about going nearer later, since he seemed to be so absorbed in the beauty. But to my horror, Grane got up and swifty started walking towards the fairies. I totally lost my senses for what felt like a half hour. When I was back, it was too late. We were in a tree trunk. It was dark and all I could see was the bark of wood all around me. The last thing I could remember was the fairies taking Grane and me to the trunk. From the corner of my eye I spotted Grane sitting in a corner. He accepted his mistake and felt sorry for putting us in trouble. It felt like I had been trapped in the worst nightmare. I thought about how neither of us had food or water, and were trapped in here forever, when suddenly I felt someone shaking me, it was mom. In a wink of my eye, everything got clearer in my head. What I had been seeing all along was a dream. I decided to tell the real Grane all about it and secretly wished that I could see those beautiful fairies in life someday, although nothing is worth getting trapped in a tree so probably not!

All Because of Albania

Tim, a thirteen year old, was forced to clean the old book shelf with his grandmother. He swept, dusted, twisted and swirled until he came across a huge book secured with a lock. Out of curiosity he went to his grandmother. He said, "Granny, what is this book about?" His grandmother smiled at him as if she was glad that Tim asked this question. "Yes, this book was gifted to me by my father. Do you want to know about it?" said the grandmother gleefully. Tim jumped out of his seat and sat close to his grandmother to hear all about it.

"Back when Albania was wild, everybody was in search of a secret passage to Albania," grandmother started. "I too was one of the people who burnt the midnight oil in search of this secret passage."

"What exactly was in Albania that made everybody go wild? Perhaps, where is Albania?" asked Tim. "Where it was," mumbled granny. "It was in the heart of woods."

Only in a knock would do.

"Only the chosen one can pass it to find out the truth." Grandmother had just finished when there was a knock on the door and Tim's mother was calling them for lunch. Tim was thinking about the story granny had told him over lunch. He thought of all the possible things that could be inside Albania: chocolate fountains, a stream with the power to call the dead one's back, magic- ust things you wouldn't believe existed.

Albania overnight became a representation of the extraordinary for Tim, and he too was lured into the quest to discover this majestic place and find what lay within it. Tim couldn't control himself and left for the forest with his dog, the next morning. He kept recalling what granny had told him while walking and stopped right in front of a huge tree when Casper (his dog) started barking. Tim calmed Casper and looked up at the tree. He could feel something in the wind calling him towards the tree trunk. Tim knocked, just as granny had mentioned. To his surprise, a long walkway came into focus. Tim and Casper went in cautiously. After walking for about five minutes in complete darkness, a huge library with old books appeared. The smell in there was so strong that Tim wanted to doze off to sleep at that very moment. He couldn't believe his eyes and thought that it was a 'mirage' but when Casper barked and moaned he came back to his senses and broke off to search for a hint of Albania.

There were thousands of books in there. Tim searched from the starting of the library to its end and stopped when his eye caught a book. It was the same old book which he had seen in his house. Thankfully, Tim had bought it with him and when he put the two together a blinding light flashed and the floor beneath them slipped and he saw what nobody had seen since ages!

About the Author

Enaya Agrawal is a 12 year - old who finds her self-expressions in creative arts of writing and classical Indian dance form - Kathak. She has won many accolades and awards for her enchanting Kathak performances on various platforms, both in India and Internationally. She participated in the ABSS's 9th Cultural Olympiad of Performing Arts-2019 (official partner of UNESCO) held in Singapore and did her country proud when she came back with a Meritorious award. Besides writing and Kathak, she also loves to sing, draw, build apps and read books. However, writing remains her first love ever since she started writing and spinning stories as a little girl. Once she puts pen to paper, ideas start flowing endlessly, transporting her to another world, making her unstoppable. "Mowa Popins and the Golden Necklace" is her first published book but this little prodigy has big dreams when it comes to following her passions. This young achiever has a lot of feathers in her cap.

www.ingramcontent.com/pod-product-compliance
Lightning Source LLC
LaVergne TN
LVHW041557070526
838199LV00046B/2008